THE CHOCOLATE MONSTER

JAN PAGE

Illustrated by Tony Ross

www.randomhousechildrens.co.uk

For My Father

THE CHOCOLATE MONSTER
A CORGI BOOK 978 0 552 56801 2

Published in Great Britain by Corgi Books,
an imprint of Random House Children's Publishers UK
A Random House Group Company

Corgi Pups edition published 1998
This Colour First Reader edition published 2013

1 3 5 7 9 10 8 6 4 2

Copyright © Jan Page, 2013
Illustrations copyright © Tony Ross, 2013

The Random House Group Limited supports the Forest Stewardship Council (FSC®),
the leading international forest certification organization. Our books carrying the FSC
label are printed on FSC®-certified paper. FSC is the only forest certification scheme
endorsed by the leading environmental organizations, including Greenpeace. Our paper
procurement policy can be found at www.randomhouse.co.uk/environment.

Set in Bembo MT Schoolbook 21pt/28pt

Corgi Books are published by Random House Children's Publishers UK,
61–63 Uxbridge Road, London W5 5SA

www.**randomhousechildrens**.co.uk
www.**randomhouse**.co.uk

Addresses for companies within The Random House Group Limited can be found at:
www.randomhouse.co.uk/offices.htm

THE RANDOM HOUSE GROUP Limited Reg. No. 954009

A CIP catalogue record for this book is available from the British Library.

Printed in Italy.

Contents

COLOUR FIRST READER books are perfect for beginner readers. All the text inside this Colour First Reader book has been checked and approved by a reading specialist, so it is the ideal size, length and level for children learning to read.

Series Reading Consultant: Prue Goodwin
Honorary Fellow of the University of Reading

Chapter One

Lucy was always losing things. She lost her glasses and her hairbands. She lost her library books, her gym pumps and her swimming towel. She lost the laces from her trainers and the

buttons from her coat. She lost
the top of her drinking flask and
the bottom of her recorder. And
every time Lucy lost something
Mum lost her temper.

"Why don't you look after
things?" Mum would shout. "You
would lose your head if it wasn't
screwed on!"

"It's not my fault!" Lucy
would reply. "I *don't* lose things.
They just disappear!"

Lucy felt she was telling the truth. She always tried to keep her eyes on things. When she saw a button hanging off its thread she would tell herself to catch it and put it in her pocket.

But she never saw it fall! One minute it was there, the next it was gone.

And her glasses were *always* vanishing. One moment they were on her nose,

and the next — nowhere to be seen!

She had just lost her third pair of glasses that year, and it was only February.

"Where have you looked?"
asked Mum, really annoyed.

"Everywhere."

"You can't have looked *every-where*. Look in your school bag!"

Lucy looked in her school
bag. She found three chocolate
wrappers and a note she should
have given to her mother last
Wednesday, but her glasses
weren't there.

"Look in your coat pockets!"
said Dad.

Lucy looked in her coat
pockets and found the key to
her bicycle padlock, which she
had lost the other week, but
no glasses.

"Lucy Locket lost her pocket!" sang her brother Matthew.

"I haven't lost my pocket! You *can't* lose a pocket!"

"*You* could!" replied Matthew, dancing round the room. "Lucy Locket! Lucy Locket!"

"Look in the sitting room"
tried Mum.

But the glasses were not in the

sitting room — not down the side
of the sofa, not beside the video,
not under the television guide

and not under the rug.

"Look in the kitchen!" said Dad.

Lucy knew her glasses were not in the kitchen but she went to look anyway. She pulled out the washing machine and found a dirty sock. She looked behind

the breadbin and found some old cornflakes and three raisins.

Then she got down on her tummy and peered under the fridge. She found a fork, two shrivelled peas and a fridge magnet, but still no glasses.

"Why are you always losing things?" shouted Dad crossly. "Matthew never loses anything!"

Matthew gave a smug smile. He followed Lucy from room to room, chanting, "Lucy Locket lost her pocket! Lucy Locket lost her pocket!"

"I tell you they've disappeared!" Lucy said at last.

"No they haven't! Things don't just vanish into thin air!" cried Mum.

Mum was right. Things didn't just vanish into *thin air*. They

went somewhere. And Lucy
wished she knew exactly where
that somewhere was.

Chapter Two

After a few days Mum took
Lucy to the opticians to order yet
another new pair of glasses. The
optician was not very pleased.
Nor was Mum.

"Try wearing them round your neck on a chain," said the optician.

So Mum bought Lucy a gold chain and hooked the frame of her new glasses onto either end. When they weren't on her nose, the glasses sat on Lucy's chest where she could keep an eye on them.

And it seemed to work! For
a whole month Lucy managed
not to lose her glasses. From the
moment she woke up she put the
chain round her neck and she
didn't take it off until she went
to sleep.

"You look stupid! You look like
a little old lady!" teased Matthew.

"Leave me alone!" cried Lucy.

"I bet you a whole week's pocket money you lose those glasses!"

Lucy went for Matthew, but he skipped out of the way.

"Lucy Locket lost her pocket! Lucy Locket lost her pocket!" he teased.

Lucy chased him up the stairs and into the bedroom. She picked up her pillow and tried to bash him over the head. But Matthew leapt onto the bed and bounced out of her way, chanting his favourite rhyme.

"Lucy Locket lost her pocket!"
"Get lost! You're the most
horrible brother in the world!"
Matthew jumped off the
bed and ran off laughing. Lucy
sat down and burst into tears.

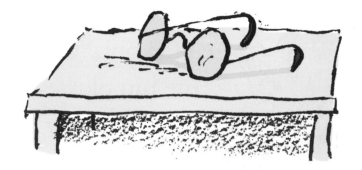

Crying made her glasses steam up so she took them off and went to find a tissue.

She only left them for a moment, but a moment was all that was needed. When Lucy came back the glasses had vanished!

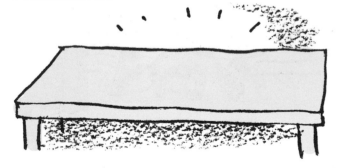

 "Matthew!" she called out. "Give me my glasses back, I know you've got them!" But Matthew had gone into the garden to play football. He couldn't have taken the glasses. So where had they gone?

Lucy looked everywhere. She looked under her pillow and behind the curtain. She looked on the top of her wardrobe and in the bottom of her toy-box.

She emptied all her drawers and took off all the bedclothes. The room looked a terrible mess and she still hadn't found her glasses!

Then she spotted something shining on the carpet. It was the gold chain, poking out from under the bed. So that's where they were!

Lucy got down and crawled on her tummy. It was very dark

and dusty under there. She found a ruler, an old vest and six felt pens, but — no glasses!

"Bother! Bother! Bother!" she cried, banging her fist three times on the floor.

"Come in!" said a voice. And someone — or something — lifted up a floorboard!

Chapter Three

Lucy was so shocked she banged her head on the bottom of the bed.

"Ouch!"

"Hurry up! I haven't got all day!" said the voice from under the floor.

Lucy shuffled forward and looked into the hole. It was very dark, but after a few seconds her eyes got used to the gloom. And then she could not believe

what she was seeing! Sitting on a
plastic box in the centre of what
looked like a sitting room, was a
small monster, about the size of
a rabbit.

He was very peculiar to look at, rather fat and wrinkly, with several pairs of eyes and a head that was far too big for his tiny body. He was wearing a cloak covered in hundreds of buttons, and a small crown, which looked like the silver ring Lucy had lost on her birthday. He had odd

gloves on both his hands and feet, and he was wearing three pairs of Lucy's glasses!

"Excuse me, but everything you're wearing is mine!" said Lucy.

"Not any more," said the monster. "Finders keepers, losers weepers."

"That's not fair! I don't lose things – you have been stealing them!"

"Me a thief? How dare you?" replied the monster. "I only take what you leave lying around."

"But I only put those glasses down for a second! Give them back to me – right now!"

"Never! Finders, keepers – that's the rule round here."

"Well, it's a very stupid rule," said Lucy crossly. "Who are you, anyway?"

"I am the keeper of the Lost Property Cupboard. Every house has a Lost Property Cupboard, didn't you know?"

Lucy shook her head. "We have a Lost Property Cupboard at school, but they don't keep things for ever," she replied. "If you've lost something you can go to the Lost Property Cupboard and *get it back!*"

"Well, it doesn't work like that here. I put everything you lose to good use. And a rather splendid job I've made of this place, don't you think?"

Lucy looked around her. It *did* look warm and cosy, and there was something about the room that was rather familiar . . .

The room was lit by the beam
of a torch which stood in the
corner. And now she looked
closely, Lucy could see that the
walls were papered with letters
typed on white paper – school

letters! The chairs were plastic
lunchboxes and the table was a
stack of library books. There was
a vase made from the bottom of
a recorder and a camera which
sat in the corner like a television.

The carpet was bright and stripy with a picture of a fish. It was an old swimming towel! At the back of the room was the monster's bed. It had handkerchiefs for sheets and a great pile of hats and scarves for blankets. In fact,

everything in the room had once belonged to Lucy. Here were all the things she had ever lost in her life!

"Why do you only take *my* things?" she asked.

"Because I live under your bed, of course," replied the monster.

"That's not fair!" cried Lucy. "You keep getting me into trouble."

But the monster didn't seem to care too much about that.

"There's only one thing you look after properly. Only one thing you never, *never*, leave lying around."

"Really?" said Lucy, surprised. "What's that?"

"The chocolate bars you buy with your pocket money." The

monster gave a huge, longing sigh. "Oh, I so love chocolate! Every time you eat a bar the yummy smell drifts under the floorboards and into my room. I can hardly bear it! I creep out and watch you sitting on your bed, munching away. I keep

hoping that you'll leave a tiny piece for me. But you never do. You eat every bit. You even lick the wrapper . . . ! Oh, I'd do anything to have a whole bar of chocolate, all to myself."

Lucy thought about this for a few moments. Then she had an idea. "If I bought you a bar of chocolate, would you give me back some of my things?"

"A *whole* bar?" he asked.

"Of course."

"Yes! Yes! Yes!" The monster smiled and licked his lips.

"Great . . . !" cried Lucy, and
she gave him a list of what she
needed most, including, of course,
her new glasses. Then Lucy had
another, even better, idea.

"How many bars of chocolate would it take for you to move *out* of my room and *into* somebody else's?" she asked, with a twinkle in her eye.

"Just one," replied the monster.

"But it would have to be one of those enormous giant-sized bars of thick milk chocolate with 144

squares! You know, like the one
you had for your birthday. Give
me a chocolate bar like that and
I will move anywhere you like!"

"Then it's a deal!" laughed
Lucy, and she shook his fat,
wrinkly hand.

Chapter Four

That afternoon Lucy went to the shops and spent her pocket money on an enormous giant-sized bar of thick milk chocolate with 144 squares. Then, when

nobody was looking, she crept
up to her room and knocked
three times on the floor under
her bed. The Chocolate Monster
was waiting for her. And
when he saw the huge bar of
chocolate all three pairs of eyes
lit up!

"That's the one!" he cried and he gave her back everything she asked for. Then Lucy helped him pack his furniture and he moved out of her room for good.

Mum could hardly believe it
when Lucy showed her all the
things she had found: her silver
ring, her lunchbox, her camera,
the library books, two pairs of

gloves and all three pairs of
glasses.

"Where on earth did you find
them?" asked Mum.

"Under my bed," said Lucy

quite truthfully. And after
she made her deal with the
Chocolate Monster Lucy never
lost a thing.

But Matthew
started to lose
everything!
He couldn't
understand what
was happening. He lost his
pencil case and one of his shin-
pads. He lost his school reading

book and his
new waterproof
watch. He lost
the top of his

pyjamas and the bottom of his
tracksuit. He lost three footballs
in a fortnight and two pairs of
swimming trunks in a week. And
then Mum really lost her temper.

"What's wrong with you, Matthew?" she shouted. "You've become so careless!"

"Why are you always losing things?" added Dad crossly. "Lucy never loses anything."

"I *don't* lose things," Matthew shouted back. "They just disappear!"

Lucy didn't tease him or sing nursery rhymes about people losing their pockets. She just followed him round the house, with a smug smile on her face.

And every so often – *when
he wasn't being nasty to her* – she
would creep up to his bedroom
with a big bar of chocolate.

"Here we are, Matthew," she
would say later. "I found these

things under your bed." And she would give him back just a few of the things he had lost.

"Thank you," Matthew would grunt back. And he never called her Lucy Locket again.

THE END

Colour First Readers

Welcome to Colour First Readers. The following pages are intended for any adults (parents, relatives, teachers) who may buy these books to share the stories with youngsters. The pages explain a little about the different stages of learning to read and offer some suggestions about how best to support children at a very important point in their reading development.

Children start to learn about reading as soon as someone reads a book aloud to them when they are babies. Book-loving babies grow into toddlers who enjoy sitting on a lap listening to a story, looking at pictures or joining in with familiar words. Young children who have listened to stories start school with an expectation of enjoyment from books and this positive outlook helps as they are taught to read in the more formal context of school.

Cracking the code

Before they can enjoy reading for and to themselves, all children have to learn how to crack the alphabetic code and make meaning out of the lines and squiggles we call letters and punctuation. Some lucky pupils find the process of learning to read undemanding; some find it very hard.

Most children, within two or three years, become confident at working out what is written on the page. During this time they will probably read collections of books which are graded; that is, the books introduce a few new words and increase in length, thus helping youngsters gradually to build up their growing ability to work out the words and understand basic meanings.

Eventually, children will reach a crucial point when, without any extra help, they can decode words in an entire book, albeit a short one. They then enter the next phase of becoming a reader.

Making meaning

It is essential, at this point, that children stop seeing progress as gradually 'climbing a ladder' of books of ever-increasing difficulty. There is a transition stage between building word recognition skills and enjoying reading a story. Up until now, success has depended on getting the words right but to get pleasure from reading to themselves, children need to fully comprehend the content of what they read. Comprehension will only be reached if focus is put on understanding meaning and that can only happen if the reader is not hesitant when decoding. At this fragile, transition stage, decoding should be so easy that it slowly becomes automatic. Reading a book with ease enables children to get lost in the story, to enjoy the unfolding narrative at the same time as perfecting their newly learned word recognition skills.

At this stage in their reading development, children need to:

- Practice their newly established early decoding skills at a level which eventually enables them to do it automatically

- Concentrate on making sensible meanings from the words they decode

- Develop their ability to understand when meanings are 'between the lines' and other use of literary language

- Be introduced, very gradually, to longer books in order to build up stamina as readers

In other words, new readers need books that are well within their reading ability and that offer easy encounters with humour, inference, plot-twists etc. In the past, there have been very few children's books that provided children with these vital experiences at an early stage. Indeed, some children had to leap from highly controlled teaching materials to junior novels.

This experience often led to reluctance in youngsters who were not yet confident enough to tackle longer books.

Matching the books to reading development

Colour First Readers fill the gap between early reading and children's literature and, in doing so, support inexperienced readers at a vital time in their reading development. Reading aloud to children continues to be very important even after children have learned to read and, as they are well written by popular children's authors, Colour First Readers are great to read aloud. The stories provide plenty of opportunities for adults to demonstrate different voices or expression and, in a short time, give lots to talk about and enjoy together.

Each book in the series combines a number of highly beneficial features, including:

• Well-written and enjoyable stories by popular children's authors

• Unthreatening amounts of print on a page

• Unrestricted but accessible vocabularies

• A wide interest age to suit the different ages at which children might reach the transition stage of reading development

- Different sorts of stories – traditional, set in the past, present or future, real life and fantasy, comic and serious, adventures, mysteries etc.

- A range of engaging illustrations by different illustrators

- Stories which are as good to read aloud to children as they are to be read alone

All in all, Colour First Readers are to be welcomed for children throughout the early primary school years – not only for learning to read but also as a series of good stories to be shared by everyone. I like to think that the word 'Readers' in the title of this series refers to the many young children who will enjoy these books on their journey to becoming lifelong bookworms.

Prue Goodwin

Honorary Fellow of the University of Reading

Helping children to enjoy *The Chocolate Monster*

If a child can read a page or two fluently, without struggling with the words at all, then he/she should be able to read this book alone. However, children are all different and need different levels of support to help them become confident enough to read a book to themselves.

Some young readers will not need any help to get going; they can just get on with enjoying the story. Others may lack confidence and need help getting into the story. For these children, it may help if you talk about what might happen in the book.

Explore the title, cover and first few illustrations with them, making comments and suggestions about any clues to what might happen in the story.

Read the first chapter aloud together. Don't make it a chore. If they are still reluctant to do it alone, read the whole book with them, making it an enjoyable experience.

The following suggestions will not be necessary every time a book is read but, every so often, when a story has been particularly enjoyed, children love responding to it through creative activities.

Before reading

There is an element of fantasy in the story of *The Chocolate Monster* but it is also about realistic family life. Talk about Lucy's problem – she loses little things, even important ones like glasses, all the time. Lots of people (not just children) have similar irritating 'problems' (for example: forgetting to switch off the lights, put things away or shut doors). Wouldn't it be nice to find that there was a reason for irritating things happening?

During reading

Asking questions about a story can be really helpful to support understanding but don't ask too many – and don't make it feel like test on what has happened. Relate the questions to the child's own experiences and imagination.

For example, ask: 'Do you sometimes lose things?', 'Where would you look first if you lost something?' and 'Do you think the Chocolate Monster is real?'

Responding to the book

If your child has enjoyed the story, it increases the fun by doing something creative in response. If possible, provide art materials and dressing up clothes so that they can make things, play at being characters, write and draw, act out a scene or respond in some other way to the story.

Activities for children

If you have enjoyed reading this story, you could:

- Get a piece of paper and a pencil to do the Chocolate Monster Quiz. All the answers are at the start of the book:

  1. Who wrote *The Chocolate Monster* and who did the illustrations?

  2. What did Mum lose every time Lucy lost things?

  3. What did Lucy's brother, Matthew, sing when she lost things?

  4. What did Lucy find under the fridge?

- Visit www.phrases.org.uk to find out about sayings. The Monster says, 'Finders keepers, losers weepers'. Do you know this saying? Find out about different sayings on the Internet.

- Design a Chocolate Monster of your own.

- Write your own story about something that happened in your family. Make it as funny as you can so everyone will laugh and no one will feel picked on.

★ ★ ★ **COLOUR FIRST READER** ★ ★ ★
by **Sainsbury's**

CERTIFICATE
of READING

My name is

_____

I have read

_____

Date

_____

ALSO AVAILABLE AS COLOUR FIRST READERS